Adèle & Simon

Barbara McClintock

Frances Foster Books   Farrar, Straus and Giroux   New York

Adèle & Simon

Adèle picked up her little brother, Simon, at school.
Simon was waiting by the door.
He had his hat and gloves and scarf and sweater,
his coat and knapsack and books and crayons,
and a drawing of a cat he'd made that morning.
"Simon, please try not to lose anything today," said Adèle.
Simon said, "I'll try."

At the corner they stopped to talk to Madame Biscuit, the grocer.
She gave them each an apple.
After a while Simon tugged on Adèle's sleeve.

"Where's my drawing?" he asked.
They looked and looked, and looked again, but couldn't find it.
So off they went without the drawing to the park nearby.

Adèle set out their after-school snack on a park bench.
But Simon had disappeared.
Monsieur Pierre, the gardener, helped her look for him . . .
And there he was, up a tree.
"Come down this minute!" Adèle scolded.

Simon climbed down with his hat and gloves and scarf and sweater,
his coat and knapsack and crayons—but no drawing of a cat.
And where were his books?
Simon didn't even notice they were missing.
"Let's go see the dinosaurs next," he said.

Soon they were wandering happily among the fossils
and dinosaurs at the natural history museum.
They said hello to their friend Monsieur Dent, the museum guard.
Simon had his hat and gloves and sweater, his crayons and coat

and knapsack—but no drawing of a cat.

And where was his scarf?

"Simon, how can you lose things like this?" asked Adèle.

Simon shrugged his shoulders. He shook his head. He didn't know.

Adèle and Simon left the museum.
The day was bright. It felt wonderful to walk.
"Adèle," said Simon, "have you seen my glove?"

"Oh, Simon, not again!" said Adèle.
They hunted all over and couldn't find it.
But Simon wasn't worried. Maybe he didn't need two gloves
when he still had one.

They stopped to watch a puppet show.
Several of Adèle's friends were there.
The girls talked and talked until Simon interrupted.
"Adèle, I've lost my other glove."
Everyone joined the hunt. They looked under benches

and behind shrubs, but the glove wasn't found.

"Simon! We are spending the whole day looking for your things!
Don't lose anything else!" scolded Adèle.

But Simon wasn't listening. He was already on his way down the path,
following the sounds that came from the street.

Horns blew, drums boomed. It was a parade!
And right in front was their friend Paul.
Adèle and Simon walked along beside him
until they reached the art museum.

"Simon!" said Adèle. "Where's your hat?
What is Mama going to say?"
"Don't worry," said Simon. "I still have my sweater and coat
and knapsack and crayons."

Inside the museum, Simon went directly to the room with his favorite
paintings. He got out his paper and crayons and started to draw.
People politely stepped around him.
Madame Quill, his art teacher from school, was there.
Simon proudly showed her his drawing.

"You must sign it," she said.
But Simon couldn't find his crayons.
Everyone helped him look, but no crayons were found.
Simon hugged Adèle before she could scold him.
"Can we go now?" he asked. "I'm hungry."

"Oh, Simon," Adèle sighed. "You've got to stop losing things!
I'm tired of looking for hats and gloves and crayons and books
and scarves everywhere we go!"

But Simon was too busy eating éclairs and chocolates to listen.
And when it was time to go, he had entirely forgotten
where he'd put his knapsack.
"I'm sure it will turn up somewhere," said Monsieur Bonbon, the waiter.

They left the pastry shop and headed toward home.
"Oh, look, Simon. Acrobats!" said Adèle.
Harlequins juggled, a sword swallower swallowed,
and the strong man lifted with mighty effort.
All the children joined in the fun.

Simon's friend Léo was there, doing handstands and tumbling
along with Simon until they were out of breath.
"But, Simon, where's your coat?" asked Adèle.
Everyone hunted high and low,
but Simon's coat was not to be found.

Adèle was about to scold Simon again.

But Simon wasn't there.

André, the postman, helped Adèle look for him.

They finally found Simon, without his sweater.

"I was too warm," Simon explained.

Adèle sighed. "It's getting late. Let's go."

At last they were home, and Adèle was tired.
Tired of Simon losing his things.
Tired of looking for the things Simon lost.
Tired of looking for Simon.

Mama was waiting.
"Simon," said Mama, "where are your hat and gloves and scarf
and sweater, your coat and knapsack and books and crayons?"
"And the drawing of a cat he made at school," added Adèle.
Just then there was a knock at the door . . .

And there were Simon's things!

That night, after Adèle and Simon had gone to bed,
Simon asked sleepily, "Is tomorrow a school day?"
"Yes," said Adèle.
"And will you pick me up to bring me home again?" asked Simon.
"Yes," Adèle sighed.
And before Adèle could say another thing, Simon was fast asleep.

PAGES 6–7
The view looking north from the Pont-Neuf to the fashionable department store the Samaritaine, an example of the Art Nouveau style of the period.

PAGE 9
Somewhere in the fifth arrondissement.

PAGES 10–11
An old Paris street market. Scattered throughout the illustration are groupings of people based on famous pictures by the nineteenth-century artist Honoré Daumier and the early-twentieth-century photographer Eugène Atget.

PAGES 12–13
The Jardin des Plantes was established in 1635 as a royal medicinal herb garden, and later as a school of botany. There are many ancient trees in the garden, including a cedar of Lebanon that was planted in 1734. The botanist Bernard de Jussieu carefully carried the young cedar in a pot from England to the Jardin. At the end of the journey, the pot fell and broke, and Jussieu carried the precious seedling in his hat to the spot where it was planted. The Jardin also contains a zoo, a maze, and a little kiosk that is the oldest metal structure in Paris.

PAGES 14–15
The gallery of paleontology in the Muséum National d'Histoire Naturelle was built in 1898 and is considered a masterpiece of metal architecture. Its collection of large fossils and dinosaurs is arranged as an "evolutionary herd," starting with the earliest fish and moving on to dinosaurs and to animals that coexisted with prehistoric man.

PAGES 16–17
The Métro station at St-Michel. When the Paris Métro opened in 1900, a young architect, Hector Guimard, was chosen to design the entranceways. His Art Nouveau designs produced graceful metal structures suggesting natural plant forms. His idea was to brighten up the daily monotony of going to work with cheerful, whimsical designs. Not everyone greeted them with enthusiasm— one newspaper called them "galvanized zinc ichthyosaurus skeletons," another called them "dragon wings." Many of the Métro entrances were torn down before the remaining ones were protected as historic sites.

PAGES 18–19
The Jardin du Luxembourg—sixty acres of lawns, groves, tree-lined paths, statues, and formal terraces—is located in the heart of the Left Bank of Paris. A large pond in the garden is a favorite spot for sailing toy boats. There is a puppet theater, an open-air café, places to play chess and the traditional game of pitching balls called *boules*, as well as a bee-keeping school and plenty of garden chairs for sitting.

PAGES 20–21
The Musique de la Garde Républicaine, a band made up of members of the French military, evolved from military bands established by Napoléon Bonaparte. It was given its present name in 1871 and made a triumphant tour of the United States in 1872. Today it is regarded as one of the great bands of the world.

PAGES 22–23
The Musée du Louvre is the home of one of the most important art collections in the world. The Louvre began as a fortress in 1190 to protect Paris against Viking raids. The fortress was eventually replaced by a Renaissance-style

building during the reign of Francis I. Four centuries of French kings and emperors improved and enlarged the buildings to what they are today. The Louvre became a museum in 1793. A recent addition is the main entrance, a glass pyramid designed by the architect I. M. Pei. Among those helping Simon find his crayons in the illustration are the artists Edouard Vuillard, Odilon Redon, Edgar Degas, and Mary Cassatt.

PAGES 24–25
The Maison Cador is a patisserie and tea salon that faces the eastern end of the Louvre and has been serving candies, cakes, and French marzipan since the early 1870s.

PAGES 26–27
The beautiful Gothic Cathédrale de Notre-Dame stands on the site of a Roman temple. Pope Alexander III laid the first stone for the cathedral in 1163. One hundred seventy years of hard work by medieval craftsmen and architects followed before Notre-Dame was completed. The cathedral is famous for its many gargoyles, and was the setting for Victor Hugo's novel *The Hunchback of Notre-Dame*. All distances in France are measured from a point in front of the cathedral.

PAGES 28–29
The Cour de Rohan is a charming enclave of old houses in the Latin Quarter that takes its name from the archbishops of Rouen, who had a mansion there in the fifteenth century. The composer Camille Saint-Saëns was born in one of the houses in 1835.

PAGES 30–31
The interior of Adèle and Simon's home was inspired by paintings of the French painter, printmaker, and photographer Edouard Vuillard, who lived from 1868 to 1940.

To Frances

The endpaper map showing Adèle and Simon's route from school to home is from the 1907 edition of *Paris and Environs* by Karl Baedeker.

Copyright © 2006 by Barbara McClintock
All rights reserved
Distributed in Canada by Douglas & McIntyre Ltd.
Color separations by Chroma Graphics PTE Ltd.
Printed in the United States of America by Worzalla
Designed by Irene Metaxatos
First edition, 2006
3 5 7 9 10 8 6 4 2

www.fsgkidsbooks.com

Library of Congress Cataloging-in-Publication Data
McClintock, Barbara.
    Adèle and Simon / Barbara McClintock.— 1st ed.
        p. cm.
    Summary: When Adèle walks her little brother, Simon, home from school he loses one more thing at every stop: his drawing of a cat at the grocer's shop, his books at the park, his crayons at the art museum, and more.
    ISBN-13: 978-0-374-38044-1
    ISBN-10: 0-374-38044-9
    [1. Lost and found possessions—Fiction. 2. Brothers and sisters—Fiction.] I. Title.

PZ7.M47841418 Ad 2006
[E]—dc21

                                        2002035311

Legend
1. Cat Drawing
2. Books
3. Scarf
4. Right Glove
5. Left Glove
6. Hat
7. Crayons
8. Knapsack
9. Coat
10. Sweater
PALAIS DU LOUVRE
Quai du Louvre
Institut de France
Hôtel d. Monnaies
Pont Neuf
Q. de la Mégisserie
PALAIS DE JUSTICE
Sainte Chapelle
St. Germain des Prés
Marché St. Germain
St. Sulpice
Mairie
PALAIS DU LUXEMBOURG
Sénat
Musée
JARDIN DU LUXEMBOURG
Gare du Luxembourg
Ecole de Médecine
Ecole Pratique de Médecine
Lycée St. Louis
SORBONNE
Collège de France
St. Severin
R. Soufflot
Inst. Catholique
R. de Fleurus
Ecole des Mines
20
19
6

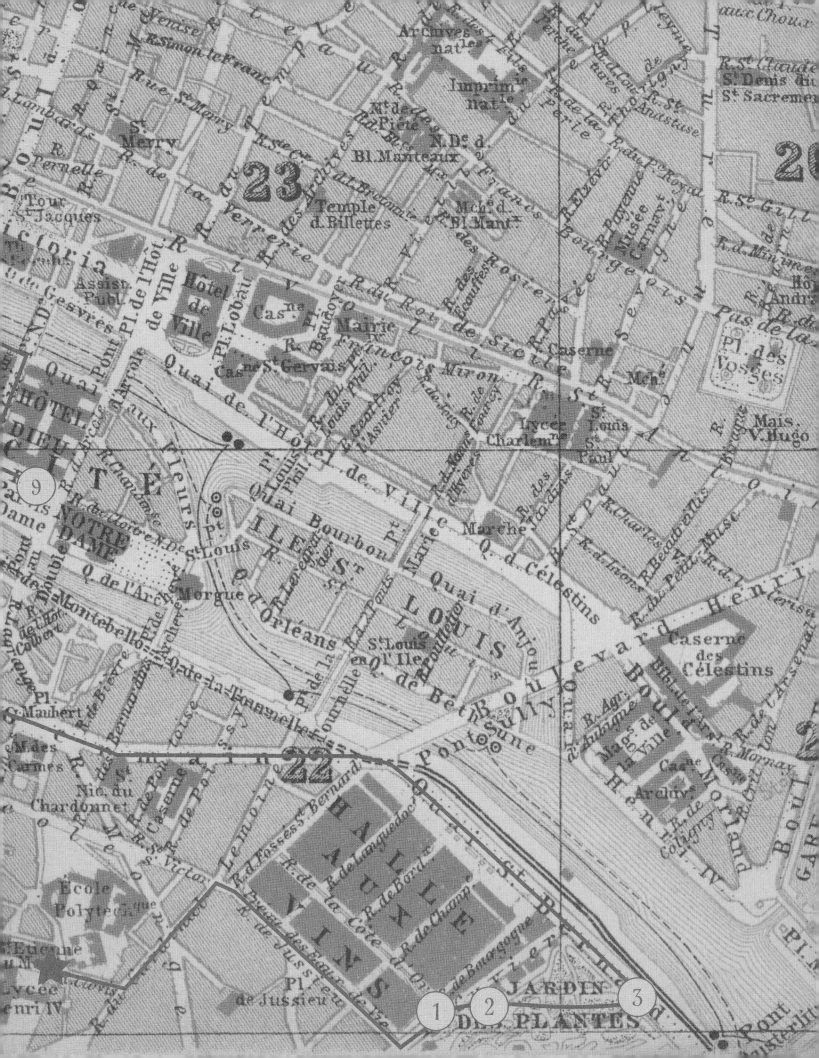